HAYNER PUBLIC LIBRARY DISTRICT ALTON
W9-AGV-647

Barbara Cohen

MAKE A WISH, MOLLY

Illustrated by Jan Naimo Jones

A Doubleday Book for Young Readers

Also by Barbara Cohen

THE CHRISTMAS REVOLUTION
THE ORPHAN GAME
MOLLY'S PILGRIM

A Doubleday Book for Young Readers
Published by Delacorte Press
Bantam Doubleday Dell Publishing Group, Inc.
1540 Broadway
New York, New York 10036

Library of Congress Cataloging in Publication Data
Cohen, Barbara.
Make a wish, Molly / by Barbara Cohen ; illustrated by Jan Naimo Jones.
p. cm.
Summary: Molly, who recently emigrated with her family from Russia to New Jersey, learns about birthday parties and who her real friends are.
ISBN 0-385-31079-X
[1. Jews—United States—Fiction. 2. Russian Americans—Fiction. 3. Birthdays—Fiction. 4. Parties—Fiction. 5. Friendship—Fiction. 6. Mothers and daughters—Fiction.] I. Jones, Jan Naimo, ill. II. Title.
PZ7.C6595Mak 1994
[E]—dc20 93-17901 CIP AC

Designed by Lynn Braswell
Manufactured in the United States of America
March 1994
10 9 8 7 6 5 4 3 2 1

For Levi, Jacob, and Yasmin

I didn't know about birthdays. In Russia we hadn't celebrated birthdays. But I learned once we came to Winter Hill.

I had started school in the fall, and I'd hated it. But by spring I didn't hate it anymore. That's because I had a friend. Her name was Emma. Her desk was next to mine.

Emma was friends with Elizabeth too. She'd been friends with Elizabeth before I moved to Winter Hill, and she still was. Elizabeth hated me. She thought Miss Stickley, our teacher, liked me better than her. In first and second grade, Emma told me, Elizabeth had been teacher's pet. We'd been studying about the queen of England in our history book. Elizabeth thought she ought to be teacher's pet in third grade too. She thought teacher's pet was a permanent position, like queen of England.

"Listen," Emma said to Elizabeth as we were leaving the school building one afternoon, "I have to pick up a package for my mother at the butcher's. Molly can walk with us."

"She doesn't live anywhere near us," Elizabeth said. "She lives downtown, in an apartment above Brodsky's Variety Store." We lived there because Papa worked for Mr. Brodsky. Elizabeth made it sound as if we lived in the garbage dump down by the railroad tracks.

"That's the point," Emma replied. "The butcher *is* downtown. So today Molly can walk with us as far as her house."

"It'll take too long," Elizabeth said.

Emma didn't bother to argue. All she said was, "I'm walking Molly. Come if you want to. Don't come if you don't want to."

Elizabeth came. She didn't feel like walking home alone. Emma skipped along between us. Elizabeth talked to Emma; I talked to Emma. We didn't talk to each other.

We walked past Winter Hill Hardware, Gaston's Ladies Wear, and Paris Fabrics. At Hocheiser's Bakery I suddenly stopped. "Look!" I cried.

Emma and Elizabeth gazed in the direction I pointed. Behind the plate glass of the bakery window stood the most amazing cake I'd ever seen. It was three layers high and covered with pink frosting. Red roses, green leaves, and lacy white curlicues decorated each layer. On top in bright red letters matching the roses was written, "Happy Birthday, Agnes."

"It's just a birthday cake," Elizabeth said.

"I think it's the most beautiful birthday cake in the world," Emma said. "Whoever Agnes is, she's very lucky."

My mother baked. She made babka and strudel and rugelach. Rugelach were my favorites.

But my mother had never decorated a cake like the one in Hocheiser's window. I didn't think anyone could do that at home. Only a bakery could do it. "It must taste like—like clouds," I said.

"Like clouds?" Elizabeth lifted her eyebrows. "Really, Molly, you are very strange. Isn't she strange, Emma?"

But Emma was still gazing at the cake. "I think I'll ask my mother if I can have a cake like that for my birthday. Then you'll both get to taste it."

"We will?" I asked.

"Of course. At my birthday party."

"Your birthday party?"

"Heavens, Molly," Elizabeth sighed. "You're not just strange, you're also a little stupid."

"I'll send you an invitation," Emma said, "in the mail."

"I've never gotten a letter in the mail." Mama and Papa did, from relatives and friends they'd left behind in Russia, but not I.

"You'll come to the party," Emma explained, "with all the other girls. We'll play pin the tail on the donkey and pick-up-sticks. Then my mother will bring out the cake, and everyone will sing 'Happy Birthday,' and I'll make a wish and blow out the candles, and we'll all eat the cake, with ice cream."

"After that comes the best part," Elizabeth added. "Emma will open her presents."

"Her presents?"

"Everyone who comes to the party has to bring Emma a present," Elizabeth laughed. "I should never have told you. Then you'd have come without a present. You'd have felt silly. That would have been a wonderful joke."

"You'll get a present too," Emma said.

"I will?" I felt as stupid as Elizabeth said I was.

"A small present. A favor, like a yo-yo or a pencil box or jacks. But you have to bring me a bigger present."

"Like what?"

"A game, maybe. Parcheesi or checkers. Or a toy. Or jewelry, or some pretty handkerchiefs. Something like that."

Elizabeth shook her head. "You people," she said. "You don't know anything."

Emma had no more errands downtown, so I didn't walk home with her and Elizabeth again. But several days later, when I ran into the house, Mama waved a pink envelope in my face. "Malkeleh!" she said. "You got a letter." Only she didn't say it in English. Mama talked to me in Yiddish.

"It must be the invitation," I said. I took it from her hand and tore it open.

"Read it to me," Mama said. She wasn't like the other mothers in Winter Hill. She couldn't speak English very well, and she couldn't read or write it at all. If Mama had to send a note to school, she asked Mr. Brodsky to write it. I hated that. Mr. Brodsky knew all our business.

The invitation was written out in an elaborate script, with lots of flourishes, but I was a good reader. I had no trouble with it. I recited it out loud, slowly:

Miss Emma DeWitt

invites

Miss Molly Hyman

to a birthday party

Thursday, April 16

at five o'clock in the afternoon

115 Mountain Avenue

Winter Hill, New Jersey

R.S.V.P.

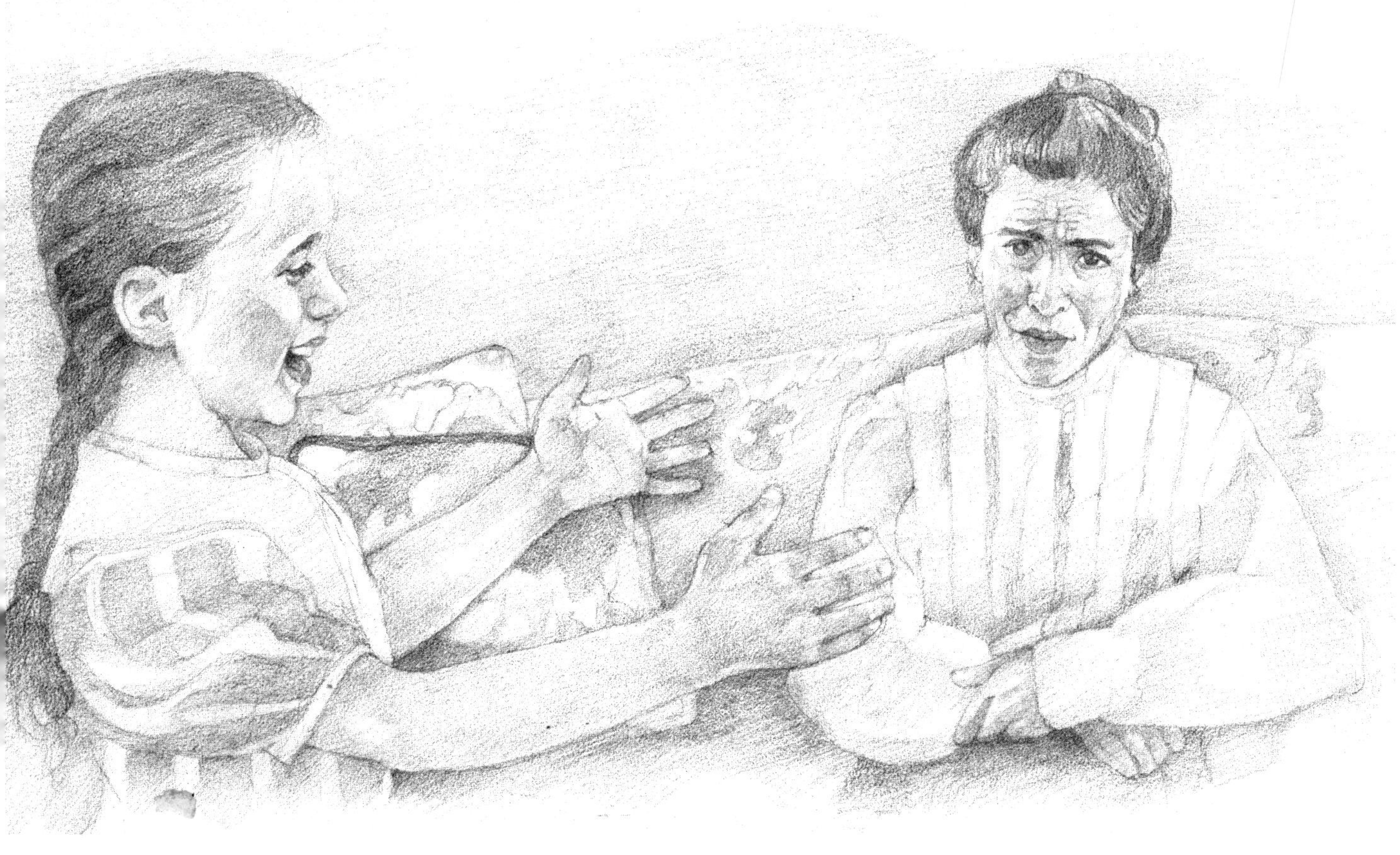

"A birthday party?" Mama asked.

I remembered every word Emma had told me. "You go to the house of the person whose birthday it is," I explained. "You play games, you give her a present, and she gives you a present."

"What's the point of that?" Mama asked. "Why don't you just each keep your own presents?"

"Oh, Mama," I said, "you just don't understand. It's an American thing. She gives you a little present, but you give her a big present. Because it's *her* birthday."

"Oh." But her face was wrinkled in a frown. She still didn't understand, not really. There was so much about America that Mama didn't understand.

"You eat ice cream and cake," I continued. "The cake is the most beautiful thing you ever saw." I was sure Emma's would be just like the one in Hocheiser's window. "It's covered with pink frosting," I explained to Mama. "It has all these little roses on it and white lace. On top there are letters that spell out 'Happy Birthday' and your name. It tastes like..." I hesitated. Maybe Elizabeth was right. Maybe "It tastes like clouds" *was* a strange thing to say. "It tastes wonderful," I declared.

"A pink cake," Mama said. "Only in America. What about the present? What does that have to be?"

"A game," I said, "or jewelry or a toy or handkerchiefs."

"Doll clothes," Mama said. "You find out the size of Emma's favorite doll and I'll make her some clothes."

"Doll clothes?" I wasn't sure they counted as a toy. And I would have liked Mama to buy a present in a store. But she was an excellent seamstress. Emma probably wouldn't be able to tell the doll clothes she made from store-bought ones. "Well, I guess doll clothes will be okay," I replied hesitantly.

"Malkeleh...what does R.S.V.P. mean?" Mama asked.

"I don't know," I admitted. "I'll find out." I'd have to ask Emma—when Elizabeth wasn't listening.

R.S.V.P., Emma explained, stood for some French words that meant, "Tell me if you're coming."

"Yes," I said, "I'm coming."

Mama finished the doll clothes well before the party. I had to admit they were beautiful—a summer dress out of white dotted swiss, a winter dress in maroon velvet, and a little plaid wool coat and hat.

"We have to wrap them in pretty paper," I said.

"That's no problem," Mama assured me. "We can get the paper downstairs. But, *shaynkeit*, there *is* a problem. A different problem."

"Bubbe and Zayde are coming to visit," I cried. They were my grandparents. "I can't go."

Mama laughed. "I never saw such a mind for imagining the worst. Even if they did come, why would that keep you from the party? You can go, all right."

"Thank goodness," I murmured.

"But you can't eat there."

"What!"

Carefully Mama laid the doll clothes in her work basket. "Next week is Passover, remember? We can't eat cereal, or bread, or cake, unless it's specially made for the holiday."

I thought I might cry. "No pink cake?"

"No nothing."

"Just this once, Mama..." I begged.

Mama shook her head. "Listen to me, *shaynkeit*. This is our first Passover in the United States. We celebrate God and Moses freeing the Jewish people from slavery."

"I know," I muttered. Thousands of years before, the Jews had rushed so quickly out of Egypt their bread had no time to rise. Ever since, during the whole week of Passover, we ate nothing containing leavening, like yeast or baking powder, which might make food expand. We didn't eat anything that hadn't been specially prepared for the holiday for fear that it might have been touched by leavening. We ate flat crackers called matzo instead of bread and used matzo meal instead of flour for baking. "Only why can't I forget about Passover for just one afternoon?" I pleaded. "We're in America now."

"We're still Jews." Mama put her arm around me. "Free Jews, instead of scared Jews, the way we were in Russia. This will be our best Passover. This year we have our own freedom to celebrate."

I saw that I would never persuade Mama to let me eat the pink cake, so I stopped talking about it. I could have asked Papa, who usually gave me whatever I wanted. But he was stricter about Jewish law than Mama was. And anyway, at the bottom of my mind, a little question unrolled itself, like a worm. If I did eat the pink cake, how would Mama even know?

The day of the party I put on my best dress. Mama had made it out of white organdy, with a pleated bodice and a blue sash. Mama brushed my hair and placed a big blue bow on the back of my head. Next, she handed me the doll clothes wrapped in flowered paper. "My little all-rightnik," she said. "You look beautiful."

Then she handed me something else. She handed me a brown paper bag.

"What's that?" I asked.

"Your matzo," she said, "with butter, just the way you like it. And some coconut macaroons."

I put the brown paper bag down on the kitchen table. "I'm not taking it."

Mama picked it up and gave it back to me. "Suppose you get hungry."

"I won't get hungry."

"But just suppose you do. Take it."

I took it. I ran out of the apartment, down the stairs, and out on the sidewalk. I was afraid that if I stayed around she'd think of something else.

I slowed down as I made my way from Main Street to Maple Street

SUGAR

to High Street to Mountain Avenue. I didn't want to get to Emma's before five o'clock.

In my hand the paper bag felt as heavy as if it were packed with stones. When I reached Emma's house, I saw no one else outside. I figured I was still early. But then I realized that was a good thing.

I walked to the house that lay two beyond Emma's. It was a big brick house set in the center of a wide lawn surrounded by a hedge. I dropped the paper bag directly into the middle of the hedge. Then I turned around and went back to Emma's.

I saw Elizabeth and Fay turning the corner. I waited until they reached the walk in front of the house. "Hello, Molly," Fay said.

"Hello, Fay," I said. "Hello, Elizabeth."

"Did you get here too early?" Elizabeth asked with a sly little smile. "Is that why you were hanging around here out front?" She ran up the walk and rapped on the front door.

Fay and I hurried after her. Emma opened the front door. "Happy birthday," Elizabeth said.

"Happy birthday," Fay and I echoed.

"Come in," Emma said. Her cheeks were pink, and her eyes [illegible]e bright with excitement. "You can put the presents on that table."

We were the first, but within the next fifteen minutes six other girls arrived. We sat in the living room, like grown-ups. Mrs. DeWitt made conversation. She asked us if our parents were well and how we were doing in school. Everyone spoke very quietly.

We played the games. Besides pin the tail on the donkey and pick-up-sticks, we played charades. That actually got quite noisy. Mrs.

DeWitt gave the winners prizes: a jump rope, a paddle with a ball attached, and a box of wax crayons. I didn't win anything, but I didn't mind. After all, I had never played those games before.

It was time for the ice cream and cake. We all went into the dining room. Pink streamers encircled the brass chandelier. In the middle of the table was a crystal bowl filled with pink and white tulips. The china plates and cups were so thin you could almost see through them. At each place was a pink paper basket filled with candy, a pink paper hat, and a pink whistle with a long tongue of paper attached to it that unrolled when you blew. A flat package wrapped in pink paper lay on each plate. That turned out to be the favor, a book of paper dolls to cut out, a different one for each of us.

At last Mrs. DeWitt carried in the cake. I had guessed right. It was a pink cake, just like the one in Hocheiser's window, decorated with red roses and white lace. Only this one said "Happy Birthday, Emma" on it. Ten burning candles circled the words, one for each of Emma's nine years and one to grow on.

Everyone sang.

Happy birthday to you,
Happy birthday to you...

I had never heard the song before, but it wasn't hard to pick up. By the third line I was singing too.

Happy birthday, dear Emma,
Happy birthday to you.

Emma shut her eyes and pressed her lips together. I supposed that was when she made her wish. Then she blew out the candles. She got them all with one big breath. Everyone applauded. "Now your wish will come true," Fay cried.

Emma made the first cut with a big silver knife. Mrs. DeWitt sliced the cake and put it on the china plates with a scoop of chocolate ice cream.

We passed the laden plates from hand to hand. When I got mine, I set it down carefully in front of me. The inside of the cake was white, with pink cream between the layers. I was lucky. I received a piece with an enormous red rose on it. I cut off a corner with the side of my fork, speared it, and lifted it toward my face. My mouth was watering.

But I couldn't put that fork between my lips. I just couldn't.

I put the fork down. I wanted to eat that cake more than anything. I had told myself that I would eat it. But it was Passover, the cake was made with flour and yeast, and I could not eat it.

I cut my slice into little pieces and moved them around on my plate. Elizabeth was seated opposite me. She ate her cake in two minutes. When she was done, she looked at my plate, and then she looked at me. "Molly isn't eating," she said. "Molly isn't eating anything."

Mrs. DeWitt leaned over me and stared at my little bits of cake floating in melted ice cream. "Don't you feel good, Molly?" she asked in a gentle voice.

"I feel fine," I said. "I'm just not very hungry."

I spoke very soft, but not softly enough. Elizabeth heard me. "I know why Molly won't eat anything," she announced in ringing tones. Everyone at the table turned toward her.

"I'm not hungry," I repeated, much louder this time.

Elizabeth acted as if she hadn't even heard me. "Jews won't eat in Christians' houses," she said. "My mother told me that. And she told me that if a Christian eats in a Jew's house, the Jew breaks the plates afterward and throws the silverware in the garbage."

"That's not true!" I cried. "That's not true."

"Then eat!" Elizabeth insisted.

I blinked back the tears that were pressing against my eyes. "I can't. It's Passover. I can only eat special foods on Passover."

Elizabeth smiled slyly. "You see," she said. "What did I tell you?"

"But you don't understand..." I wanted to explain, but how could I? It would take too long, and it was so complicated. I couldn't look into Emma's face.

"There's nothing to understand," Elizabeth retorted. "Is there?" No one said a word, not even Emma.

I stood up. "I think I had better go home now," I said. "Thank you very much for inviting me. Happy birthday." I didn't actually run out of the room, but I walked as fast as I could. I didn't worry about leaving my favor behind.

Mrs. DeWitt followed me. "Are you sure you're all right, Molly? Should I call your mother and ask her to come and get you?"

We didn't have a phone. If we ever needed one, we used the phone in the store downstairs. "I'll be fine, Mrs. DeWitt. It's not far. Thank you very much."

I opened the door and stepped out of the house. Mrs. DeWitt waited a few moments before she closed the door. At the end of the walk I heard it shut. That's when I started to cry.

I ran all the way home, sobbing out loud every foot of the way. I ran up the stairs to our apartment, threw myself down on the sofa in the living room, buried my face in the cushions, and went on crying.

My mother heard me. She came out of the kitchen, sat down on the sofa, and put her arm around me. "*Shaynkeit*, what's the matter? Didn't you have a good time at the party?"

I sat up and shrugged out of her grasp. "Oh, Mama," I sobbed, "why do we have to be different? Why can't we be like everyone else?"

"We're all different," Mama said. "In one way or another we're all different."

"Why can't we be *American*?"

"Tell me what happened, *shaynkeit*."

So I told her.

"Listen, Malkeleh," Mama said when I was done, "in eleven days it's *your* birthday. We'll invite Emma and Fay and Elizabeth and the others here for a party. Then they'll see we're not *so* different."

I put my hand on Mama's wrist and squeezed it tight. "Oh, no, Mama. No, no, no. Those girls must never come here. Never."

"Why not?" Mama asked. "It would be nice."

I could not tell her we did not have china you could see through. I could not tell her we did not have a crystal bowl full of tulips on the middle of our dining-room table. We didn't even have a dining room. We were not American.

Mama said no more about it. Friday I went back to school. Emma was already at her desk when I sat down. She didn't look up from her spelling homework.

"Are you mad at me, Emma?" I asked.

"It wasn't very nice," she said, "the way you ran out of my party. You didn't even stay for the presents."

"I know it wasn't nice. It wasn't nice of me at all," I said. "I'm sorry." I just couldn't say more than that.

"Well, it's okay," she answered.

But it wasn't okay. I didn't know what to say to Emma anymore.

Maybe she was like Elizabeth. Maybe she thought Jews broke plates and threw away silverware. Maybe Fay thought so too. Maybe they all thought so.

I stayed away from them during recess. I didn't play jump rope with them. I didn't play jacks. I didn't walk out of the building with them when school was over. Emma and I still talked some. After all, we did sit next to each other. But it wasn't the same. I didn't feel as if she were my friend anymore.

The weekend dragged by. I was as miserable as I had been in the fall. Maybe I was more miserable. Because maybe it's worse to lose a friend than never to have had one at all.

I wasn't any happier the morning of my birthday. When I awoke, I felt the same heaviness in my stomach at the thought of spending a whole day in school all by myself. I sat down at the breakfast table with the same gloomy face I'd worn since Emma's party.

"Happy birthday, Malkeleh," Papa said.

"Happy birthday, *shaynkeit*," Mama said.

I managed a small smile. "Thank you," I said.

Mama took a little package out of her apron pocket. It was wrapped in the same flowered paper she'd used for Emma's doll clothes. "Here, Malkeleh," she said. "This is for you."

"A present?" I was surprised.

"Of course, a present," Mama said. "In America there are presents."

I should have undone the package carefully, so we could use the wrappings again. But I was too excited. I tore off the ribbon and paper. Inside was a long, thin white box. I opened it up and saw a slender golden chain from which hung a tiny golden heart. "Oh, Mama," I cried, "oh, Papa, it's beautiful. It's so—so grown-up."

"It's real gold," Mama said proudly.

"Mr. Brodsky let me have it at a good discount," Papa said.

"Can I wear it?" I asked. "Or do I have to save it for special occasions?"

"It's your birthday. That's a special occasion." Mama took the necklace from my hand and fastened it around my neck. "This morning I'll bake rugelach," she said. "They'll be waiting for you when you get home from school."

I still didn't want to go to school. I wanted to stay home and help Mama bake the rugelach and then eat them with milky tea as soon as they came out of the oven.

But I went. And when I sat down in my seat, I said, "Hi, Emma."

Emma turned toward me, surprised. "Hi, Molly," she said. Then she noticed. "Oh, Molly, look at your necklace. It's so beautiful. Is it new?"

I nodded. "It's my birthday present. I just got it."

"Is today your birthday?"

"Yes."

"Happy birthday, Molly."

"Thank you, Emma."

Emma and I talked quite a lot that morning. Miss Stickley had to tell us to be quiet two different times. But I still didn't walk out of the building with her and the other girls when school was over.

I could smell the apples and cinnamon in the rugelach as soon as I opened the door. I could smell them all the way up the stairs. Actually they smelled a lot better than the pink birthday cake, which

History
arithmetic
geography
Spelling.
Physical

had no smell at all. "Mama," I said, "Emma admired my necklace so much. She said it was beautiful."

Mama hugged me. "I'm so glad. I was worried."

"Worried? About what?"

"About getting the right thing."

"Oh." I thought for a minute. "Well, it is the right thing. It's just the right thing."

I went into my bedroom to drop my books and put a pinafore over my school dress, to save it. I heard the doorbell ring. I opened my door to see who it was.

I snapped the door shut again, tore off the pinafore, threw it on the bed, and stepped out into the living room. Mama's back was to me. In front of her stood Emma and Fay and Elizabeth. Emma was carrying a package wrapped in pink paper.

"Oh," Emma exclaimed, "there you are, Molly." She hesitated a moment and then thrust the package toward me. "Happy birthday."

I was so amazed it was a few moments before I could speak. When I recovered my tongue, all I could say was something really silly. "You brought me a present."

"Yes. Take it."

"But why?"

"It's your birthday, isn't it?" Fay remarked.

Emma pressed the package into my hand. "You gave me the best present I got for my birthday," she said. "My doll is so fashionably dressed now, Mama says her picture ought to be in the *Ladies' Home*

Journal. When I went home for lunch, I told Mama we had to get you a present for your birthday. She said of course, so here it is."

"I wanted to say happy birthday," Fay announced, "even if I don't have a present. So I came too. Happy birthday, Molly."

"Thank you, Fay." I looked at Elizabeth. She didn't say anything. She just smiled her sly little smile. I knew why she had come. She'd come to see if our floors were dirty and if the stuffing was coming out of our furniture. She must have been terribly disappointed, but she was careful not to show it.

I opened the package. Inside was a book. It was called *A Child's Garden of Verses* by Robert Louis Stevenson, and I could tell from the cover that it would be full of pretty pictures. "I know you like to read," Emma said.

"Oh, Emma, thank you very much," I replied. "It was very nice of you to bring me a present. I'm not even having a party."

"You're having a party," Mama said. "You're having a party right now! Do you girls like rugelach?" Her thick Yiddish accent did not seem to prevent the girls from understanding her.

"We don't eat foreign foods," Elizabeth said.

Emma spoke at the same moment. "What's rugelach?"

Mama shrugged, her hands outstretched. "They're fat, crescent-shaped pastries," I explained, "stuffed with apples, raisins, and nuts."

"Is the wonderful smell in this house rugelach?" Fay asked.

I nodded.

Fay licked her lips. "I eat rugelach."

"Me too," said Emma.

Mama clapped her hands. "You don't have to plan a party in advance," she said. "It's a party just because friends are together. Come into the kitchen, girls."

We sat down at the table. Mama took plates, cups, and saucers out of the cupboard. "After we eat off these plates and drink from these cups," she said, "Molly will carry them to the sink and I will wash them. We will all be able to eat from them again."

Emma and Fay lowered their eyes. Elizabeth didn't. She just tossed her curls.

Mama took one of the Sabbath candles she lit on Friday nights and placed it in the middle of the tray piled high with rugelach. She lit the candle and carried the tray to the table. "So, sing," she ordered.

I flushed a bright red. But Emma and Fay laughed and started to sing.

Happy birthday to you,
Happy birthday to you...

Mama poked Elizabeth's shoulder. She poked her hard. Elizabeth joined in.

Happy birthday, dear Molly,
Happy birthday to you.

Then they sang it all over again.

"Blow out the candle," Emma said. "Don't forget to make a wish first."

I had a friend named Emma. Maybe I even had another friend named Fay. I had a necklace with a gold heart. I had a mama who couldn't speak English very well but knew what to do about people like Elizabeth anyway. What was there to wish for? Under my breath I whispered, "I think Mama will always know what to do. I hope Emma and Fay are my friends forever." And then I blew out the candle.

I had not thought that Mama was very smart, but I found out that day that she was. There's more to being smart than speaking English well. Maybe Mama could not make a pink cloud cake, but she could make wonderful rugelach. No one else could make rugelach like Mama could. There was no one like my mama.